Sydney

The Wandering Sardine

Sydney
The Wandering Sardine

By Helen Howard

Edited by Doris Berdahl

Illustrated by Lloyd Kinnee

GLENWOOD PRESS
Mill Valley, California

Published by GLENWOOD PRESS
607 Glenwood Avenue
Mill Valley, CA 94941

Cover and Text Design: Lorena Laforest
Cover Art and Illustrations: Lloyd Kinnee

Library of Congress Cataloging in Publication Date
Howard, Helen
Sydney, The Wandering Sardine
I. Title.
Library of Congress Catalog Card
Number: 95-94481
ISBN: 0-9646546-0-1

First Printing
Printed in the United States of America

*Dedicated to
all children who love to
gaze out to sea and imagine
the many creatures who live
beneath its surface.*

Contents

Acknowledgments   xi

1 Heading South   1

2 Harry to the Rescue   9

3 In the Fishermen's Net   17

4 Escape !   25

5 In the Cave of the Dolphin   37

6 The Great Tidal Wave   51

7 The Shark Trails His Prey   65

8 Meeting up with Mitzi   75

9 Piggybacking on Danny   84

10 Sydney Has an Idea   92

11 Great White Meets His Doom   102

12 Back with the Family   110

Acknowledgments

My deep appreciation to the members of Scribes, a writers' group which meets regularly at Book Passage, an independent book store in Corte Madera, California, for their advice, support, and detailed critiques of my work in progress.

Thanks too, to my many friends who read various drafts of this book—in particular, Ann McCabe, Patricia Garlan, Margaret Clark, Lorraine Baker, Mary Clark Greer, Ellen Schaefer, and Dr. Kay Taylor. I am particularly in debt to Roger Rapaport of RDR Books, Berkeley, California, for his expert guidance.

Finally, my special gratitude to the teachers and children of the third and fourth grade classes in the Mill Valley elementary schools who graciously listened to the story and gave me feedback from the perspective of the age group for which it was written.

1

Heading South

The little sardine was lost somewhere in the great big ocean, and he was very scared. He'd gotten separated from his family. He'd called and called for his mother and father. He'd searched everywhere for his brothers and sisters. But they'd disappeared.

The ocean's rough waves threw him back and forth, up and down, and round and round. The water became dark and cloudy and he couldn't see anything. He grew so weak and tired he could barely move his fins. He drifted down, down, down toward the ocean floor.

Surely, thought the little sardine, this is the end of me.

But he was lucky. Close by a mother herring happened to be searching for food for her hungry young ones. When she saw the little creature floating round and round, his little fins dangling sadly in the water, she was sure he was in trouble. He did look different from her own shiny green and brown little herring children. His body was covered with silvery black scales. But this didn't worry her. Her kind heart went out to him anyway.

She swam right over, grabbed one of his fins in her mouth and pulled him along. In a sweet voice she said, "Don't be afraid. You look as if you're lost. Well, never mind. You can stay with me and my family until we find yours. My name is Silver Queen."

The little sardine was so tired out, and Silver Queen's touch so soft and loving, he felt better right away.

Later that afternoon, Silver Queen and her husband, Big Daddy, decided to search for the little sardine's family. They looked everywhere—behind big mounds of rocks, under long wavy strands of seaweed, and all over the sandy ocean floor. But a family of sardines was nowhere to be found.

"Not to worry," Silver Queen told the little sardine. "Surely they'll turn up in a day or two."

Until then, she added, she and Big Daddy would adopt him. He would become part of their family. They would name him Sydney.

✳

Sydney was sent to play among his many new brothers and sisters. And so the summer passed happily. But one day autumn came, and most mornings the sun hid behind thick clouds. The ocean changed from bright blue to dull gray, and its waters turned cold and rough.

One chilly morning, Big Daddy said it was time to pay a visit to his good friend, a wise old fish named Fred Flounder. Even though Fred had a funny flat shape and eyes on only one side of his face, Big Daddy trusted his advice. Fred could always tell when winter was coming on.

Every year, when he gave the sign, the large schools of herring and sardines prepared to swim south. They set out for warmer waters, along with many other fish in the ocean, and didn't come back until spring. They called it the Big Migration.

*

Fred was pleased to see Big Daddy. "Hi, there," he said. "Bet you want to know if it's time to head south. Gettin' a bit chilly for you, eh? Wait here just a sec. I'll swim to the top of the ocean, take a look at the sky and the waves and check out the wind."

Fred hadn't been gone but a minute when he came back. "Yup," he said, twitching his flat body back and forth. "It's time, all right. Thick clouds in the sky and a sharp bite to the wind. You better get a move on."

4

Big Daddy thanked his old friend, and he and Sydney hurried back to their family. Big Daddy called everyone together— hundreds of herring children spread out as far as the eye could see.

"Pay attention now," he said in a ringing voice. "This is important. We must get ready to swim south. Once we're there, the sun will shine all day long, the water will be nice and warm, and there'll be lots of fresh plankton and brine shrimp to eat."

There would be dangers along the way, Big Daddy warned. Big fish like to eat little herring and sardines. Especially the hungry mackerel—or even worse—the Great White Shark, which zooms through the waters without a sound and gobbles up small fish.

"But the greatest danger of all," said Big Daddy in his very sternest voice, "will come from above the sea. You must keep far away from the big boats that throw nets into the water. They can capture hundreds of fish at one time and sell their catch to the markets. So, dear children, keep your eyes open. Don't

look to the right or to the left. Above all, stay
with the family!"

So the great migration began. At a signal
from Big Daddy, the many families of the
Pacific herring and sardine clans began their
long trip south.

As they started forward, Sydney thought
he heard a faint rumbling sound, somewhere
overhead. Was that the kind of sound that
came from a boat? He trembled at the thought.
Maybe it was just his imagination. Anyway,
he decided to swim closer to a strong, young
herring named Harry, whom he'd come to
think of as his big brother. If there was any
danger, he felt Harry could protect him.

Bright sunlight flowed through the ocean
waters and sparkled on the sharp, pointed
rocks pushing through the ocean floor. Long
ropes of green and brown seaweed, thick with
leaves and berries, spun around tiny stones
and pebbles.

Sydney could see that the big flowing ocean was full of every kind of drifting creature. Each was a different color, shape, or size. Silvery shrimp lit up the dark waters with a soft glow. Dark gray clams hid in rugged half-moon shells. Spiny blue and white starfish bobbed lazily through the shadows. Sea urchins flexed long spines and padded about with tube feet. Bright, green sea robins trailed their feelers, searching for food.

Sydney was eager to see everything up close. Most of all, he longed to see what lay above the water. Forgetting about Big Daddy's warnings, he swam away from the line of fish and headed straight up to the surface of the ocean.

He could still see his big family swimming below and was sure he could return to them any time. But he soon forgot about them when two sea otters with sleek brown coats swirled close by, chasing each other in circles and touching noses. Then a pair of squid darted past him, blowing jets of water from the funnels on the sides of their heads.

Right after that, a great soft creature, covered with thick yellow scales, wandered into view. It stared at Sydney out of narrow slits. Were those his eyes? Sydney swam up for a closer look. The creature blinked and drifted away.

But by then, he'd spotted a turtle. All he could see at first was its shell, covered with brown and green markings. He swam around it. Suddenly out popped a small round head. It stared at Sydney for a second, stuck out its tongue and grabbed a tiny shrimp. Then it pulled its head back under its big shell, waved its flippers, and moved off into a rope of seaweed.

Sydney guessed it was time to get back to his family. He peered down through the ocean. All he could see now was clear, blue-green water. Where were they? He looked up and down, to the right and to the left. No family in sight! He was lost!

Worse still, a huge, dark fish had darted out of the shadowy water. It had a high, sharp back and a thick throat. Its great gills pulsed and throbbed. And one cold black eye stared straight at him.

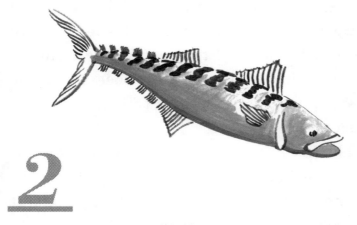

2

Harry to the Rescue

Sydney didn't like the look in that eye. This had to be the mackerel he had been warned about. Dark blue stripes swept along its back. Long, pointy teeth glowed in its open jaw. It smacked its lips and a stream of bubbles floated out of its mouth.

In his fright, Sydney tumbled, lost his balance and spun around in a circle. But just as the mackerel lunged toward him, a much larger creature—a gray and white monster—

flashed out of the shadows. It attacked the mackerel with long, jagged teeth. The two thrashed about in a wild frenzy.

Sydney watched in horror. The mackerel put up a fierce fight, trying desperately to save its life. Several times it seemed almost finished, but finally it tore loose from the monster's jaws and shot up to the surface of the ocean.

The big gray and white creature was furious. It jerked up and down, flapped its tail, and snapped its jaws. Then it swirled about and took off after the mackerel.

From his hiding place, Sydney shuddered. By now he had guessed what this was. It was the Great White Shark, feared by every living creature in the ocean! Big Daddy had often warned of the Great White—especially this one with the long, jagged scar. The scar zigzagged from his great curving mouth to his left gill slit. He must have been in many fights to have such a cruel looking wound.

Too frightened to move, Sydney drifted along near the surface of the ocean. The last light of day flickered weakly on the rolling

10

sea. He tried to stretch his fins so he could swim. But it was no use. He could go no further.

A stream of hungry seagulls swooped across the darkening sky, squawking loudly in the evening air. Sydney pointed his head downward, hoping to slide to the ocean floor and hide among the rocks. He knew a swift gull with sharp eyes and a pointy beak could dart down and swallow him in a flash!

But he was too weak to move. "Oh," he groaned, "what shall I do?" The big waves were pushing him along in full view of the gulls. Closing his eyes, he prayed for a miracle to save him.

And his prayers were answered! He heard a voice. In a flash, a silver bullet tore through the sea toward him.

"Sydney, is that you?"

The bullet whooshed to a halt. It was Harry! His big, strong brother. He had come back to save him.

"I hoped you'd find me," Sydney cried.

"Been looking for you most of the day!" Harry exclaimed. "Thought I saw you once, but it was some other dumb sardine. Good thing I promised Mother to watch out for you, or you'd stay lost! And good riddance! Dawdle and play and dream all day. That's all you do, you little twit!"

"It was that big mackerel!" Sydney blubbered. "And then a big shark . . . and . . . and . . . I nearly got eaten up!"

"Wish you had!" Harry sighed. "Well, come along with me. It's almost dark. Who knows where the family is by now? Guess we'll have to find them tomorrow."

Sydney thought he saw Harry smile— just a little. Then he was sure of it.

"It's O.K., kid," Harry said, nudging him playfully. "Cheer up. I found you, didn't I? Right now we have to find a safe place to sleep."

Flipping his dorsal fin, Harry called, "Now follow me." Sydney did as he was told, and together they darted downward, seeking safety on the rock-strewn ocean floor.

Harry knew how to dodge pokey turtles, prowling swordfish, razor-edged reefs, and strangling seaweed.

Finally, after twisting and turning for what seemed like a long time, Harry spotted a large conch shell stuck in a crevice between two rocks.

"Jeehosophat!" he cried. "We've lucked out. It's empty! Swim in, boy. Time for a rest."

Sydney didn't need to be told twice. He snuggled right into the shell's white interior. He ached all over. What a day! It was wonderful to feel safe again.

Meanwhile, all that long day their family had been swimming steadily south, thinking Sydney and Harry were right behind them. They'd kept up a brisk pace. Sometimes they'd skimmed over the frothy waves. Other times they'd moved steadily under water. So when the sun finally dropped below the horizon, they had traveled many miles.

Big Daddy called out that it was time for a rest. "A good meal will make us all feel better," he told Silver Queen. "Let's send some of the bigger boys out to catch our dinner. Harry knows where to find the best plankton."

Silver Queen hurried back to the end of the line. "Harry!" she cried. "Oh, yoo-hoo, Harry! Where are you? Time for dinner! The children are tired and hungry!"

No answer. She waited, then swam among her restless children. "Have any of you seen your big brother Harry?"

They all shook their heads. No one had seen Harry since early morning.

Then Silver Queen noticed that Sydney was gone, too. "Oh dear!" she exclaimed. "Where is our little Sydney? I don't see him anywhere." She was so upset, she started to cry.

"Now, now, my dear," Big Daddy said, coming alongside her. "We will surely find them. You know how smart our Harry is. He knows his way around the sea."

14

But Silver Queen insisted. "We just have to find them, if it takes all night!"

And so for the rest of that long night, Big Daddy and Silver Queen roamed the ocean. Starlight shimmered down on the waves, helping to light their way. They kept calling and calling for the two missing boys. But there was no answer. Harry and Sydney were nowhere to be found.

Sydney and Mitzi meet in the fishermen's net.

3

In the Fishermen's Net

Meanwhile, back in the conch shell, a sharp poke jolted Sydney awake.

"Wake up, sleepyhead!" Harry said. His glistening scales shook and shimmered in the morning light. "If we want to catch up to our family, we've got one long swim ahead of us." He opened and closed his mouth. "Boy, I'm really hungry!" He flipped out of the conch shell and disappeared into the sea. "Be right back!"

Sydney's fins still drooped. Not a bit of strength. He wondered how he'd be able to keep up with fast-swimming Harry. He thought about Silver Queen, Big Daddy, and the rest of his big family. He really missed them. Were they looking for him? he asked himself.

Harry returned, pushing a large glob of fresh plankton and a nest of squirming brine shrimp. "Eat up!" he said, swallowing a mouthful. "You'll need your strength today!"

Sydney gobbled his breakfast. He felt stronger. He gazed fondly at his smart brother who could always find good things to eat.

"Ready, boy?" Harry's voice was strong. He swished his tail back and forth and stretched his fins. "Now promise you'll stay close behind me. No wandering. You hear?"

"I promise," Sydney said and really meant it. He never wanted to get lost in the big ocean again.

Harry headed south, shooting forward by slapping his tail up and down for speed. Sydney tried to do the same. The clear, cold water gave him energy and he managed to keep Harry in sight.

The morning passed quickly. The sun rose in the sky and threw shafts of light into the sea. After three or four hours of steady swimming, Sydney paused for a brief rest, being careful not to dawdle. But as the day wore on, and Harry kept up his fast swimming, he noticed that the distance between them increased. Soon Harry was only a tiny speck far ahead. Then Sydney could no longer see him. Surely, he thought, Harry would come back. He turned on his back to float.

As he drifted and waited, he noticed a strange new thing. He'd never seen a sea creature like this one. It billowed out all over, flowed this way and that, and cast beautiful designs in the water.

He moved closer—just for a second, he promised himself. But suddenly, it was too late! He was inside the thing, pressed against hundreds of other fish—sardines, herring, a squid or two, a frightened baby turtle, and a fierce crab who attacked him with sharp claws.

"Please, please don't hurt me!" Sydney cried, trying to escape the sharp claws. This was terrible! Where was he?

"Don't mind the old crab," someone said in a soft, sweet voice.

"What?" Sydney choked.

"He's nervous and scared," the voice said.

"Who are you?"

"A sardine. Just like you. I got caught today, too." A little fish with black and silver markings and bright eyes wriggled toward him. "By the way, my name is Mitzi."

"Wha . . . what is this place?" Sydney quavered.

"You mean you don't know? It's a big fishing net. If we had any sense, we'd not be in here. But it circled around me so fast I couldn't escape."

"A net?" Sydney gasped. How could he have gotten caught after all those warnings from Big Daddy?

"Don't be so upset," Mitzi tried to comfort him. "Some of us will escape. An old herring once told me he'd escaped fishermen's nets at least two different times. When the net is pulled up out of the water, you jump as high as you can! Try real hard to flip over the side of the boat and back into the ocean."

A flutter of hope beat in Sydney's little chest.

"Besides," Mitzi continued in a more serious tone, "the net is really a protection."

Protection? This was hard to believe.

Mitzi nodded. "While we're in here the big fish can't attack us. So you see, we're safe for a little while at least."

Sydney thought she might be right. No big old mackerel or shark could get at him now. But he was still so miserable!

Then he noticed a young herring staring right at him. He looked just like . . . But no, it couldn't be. Harry would not let himself get caught in a net!

Sydney started to cry.

"Why are you crying?" Mitzi asked.

"My big brother . . . and my family!" Sydney wailed. "I'll never see them again!"

"Nonsense!" Mitzi said in a sharp voice. "That's a poor attitude. You must be hopeful.

And concentrate on escaping. Maybe we can find a small hole in the net that we can squeeze through."

Sydney had to admit this was good advice. He stopped crying and struggled to push his way through the pack of other fish. It wasn't easy. None of them wanted to move, even if they could. He thought about giving up. But Mitzi stayed right behind him, urging him on.

"Don't give up!" she gasped. "Keep trying."

Sydney finally fought his way to a rough criss-cross of ropes. The net! He was excited to see one tiny hole. But it was too small to wriggle through, even for him. Oh dear, he would never escape!

Suddenly, over the uproar of the crying, moaning fish, a voice from outside the net called his name. "Sydney! Hey, Sydney, are you in there?" Could that be Harry? Sydney couldn't believe it.

A shadow darted excitedly toward the net, right where Sydney was clinging.

"I'm in here! I'm in here!" Sydney yelled.

"You little rascal!" Harry shouted. "I've been traipsing up and down this ocean for hours. When I saw this old net I just knew you were in it!"

"Please . . . please get me out of here," Sydney begged.

"It's not so easy," Harry snorted.

"What shall I do?" Sydney wailed.

"I'll try to think of something," Harry said and shot off into the shadowy water.

✳

The deep rumble of a motor vibrated overhead. Sydney stared up in horror. For the first time since his capture, he noticed the dark underside of a boat bobbing directly above them.

"Ready, Jim?" a man's rough voice bellowed over the slap of waves against the boat. "Looks like we got one big catch today!"

"Right you are! O.K., let's pull 'em in!" another voice bellowed.

The hundreds of captured fish were quickly flattened against each other. The bulging net surged upward, dragged by a force which Sydney couldn't see.

"This is it!" he moaned. "This is really the end of me!"

But at that instant, just as the bulging net was reaching the top of the sea, Harry flashed by. "When this thing opens," he shouted, "Jump as high as you can! Hear me?"

Sydney heard. But could he jump? The sobbing baby turtle was on top of him. The crab's sharp claws dug into him. A whole lot of fish were pressing against him.

"Have courage," Mitzi choked, still clinging to his left fin.

The net was dragged to the ocean's surface. Up he went, water flowing past him. Then he was jerked over the boat's railing into the burning heat of the sun. Men's voices bawled into the wind. Rubber boots thumped on the wet, slimy deck. Dead fish lay everywhere.

Sydney could not breathe. His little body began drying up in the glare of the sun.

4

Escape!

Rough hands pounced, snatched, and grabbed at the desperate fish. Those who were caught were flung into large, slimy bins lashed to the deck. "Into the bins, you little devils!" a coarse voice rang out.

"Get them jumpers first!" another voice yelled.

Through bleary eyes, Sydney saw two giant creatures in high rubber boots. One of them, covered with the scales of dead fish,

Sydney and Harry make their break.

dove and slashed at those that were still wriggling. Waving a long knife, its blade glinting in the bright sun, he stomped and slid after those that tried to hurl themselves over the railing.

"Think you can hold out?" a voice trembled in Sydney's ear.

Sydney opened his blurry eyes. Harry lay next to him. "Harry!" Sydney managed. "How did you . . . ?"

"I am trying to save your life," Harry croaked, barely able to speak. "I grabbed the net and got dragged up with you. We gotta move fast, kid, or we're done for."

"But how . . . how . . . " Sydney asked, his voice a bare whisper.

"Only one way. Now listen to me. I'll try to flip us over the side. O.K., hold on!"

Harry slid his strong body under Sydney and arched his back. Then with a quick thrust he straightened out. Sydney flew through the air and soared over the side of the boat, with Harry right behind him!

The ocean was blissfully cool. Sydney, by this time, was so weak and his body so dried up that he could only drift downward. But Harry stayed with him. Together they sank to the sandy, rock-strewn ocean floor. Far above them now, like a dark and hungry sea monster, the fishing boat bobbed up and down. Sydney thought of Mitzi and wished she was here with him.

"How're you doin', little brother?" Harry asked, rolling about and letting the water soak into him.

"I'm O.K. now," Sydney replied, and gave his brother a big grin.

"We really escaped, didn't we?" Harry chuckled. "Now no more fooling around and getting caught in traps. Take my advice, Syd. You gotta keep an eye out for all kinds of danger. Unless you want to end up in a jar, on a shelf somewhere. You know, pickled and packed in onions and vinegar."

Sydney didn't understand. But one thing he did know by this time. You could learn something every day in this ocean. Mackerels. Sharks. Fishing nets. Getting packed in a jar. Who knows what else could happen? He'd be sure to be careful from now on.

28

"Now then," Harry was saying, "let's get as far away from that boat as we can. But first, we need to know where we are. We're kind of lost."

Sydney followed Harry to the surface of the ocean. They poked their heads out of the water. The boat was nowhere in sight. The setting sun cast long golden shadows on the water. The evening star shimmered in the sky.

Harry began to figure their location. "Let's see," he said, "south is where we're heading, so we have to find the North Star and go in the opposite direction."

While Harry searched the sky, Sydney floated happily on his back. He wondered if Mitzi had escaped. He thought about his family. His eyes slowly closed. But then, when he was almost asleep, he noticed a large shadowy thing moving swiftly toward him. It was almost upon him, in fact, before he could warn Harry.

Finally, he found his voice. "Harry! Come here quick!"

"Don't bother me," Harry said.

"Better turn around and look! Now!" Sydney shouted.

Harry took his eyes away from the sky and looked. "Hey!" he exclaimed. "We have a visitor. A dolphin, and a handsome one, too!"

The dolphin shifted its gleaming white body and moved gracefully toward them. "Greetings, friends," he said in a rumbling but pleasant voice. He winked and flapped his broad tail. His eyes shone with a friendly gleam.

"Evening, sir," Harry answered, waving his right fin in a cordial salute. "My name is Harry, son of Silver Queen and Big Daddy of the Pacific Herring Clan. And this is my youngest brother, Sydney."

The dolphin smiled at Sydney, who looked nervous. "Don't be afraid, little one," the big creature said gently. "It's true, I've eaten lots of herring and sardines in my day, but not any more. I have found they're nice, friendly little folk who mind their own business. Just as I do. We've all got an equal right to live in this big old ocean."

Sydney breathed a sigh of relief.

"Actually, it's very nice to meet up with you two," the dolphin continued sociably. "Gets mighty lonesome around here sometimes. Where you folks headin'?"

"South," Harry replied.

The dolphin looked sad. "Winter migration, eh? Everybody's on the move these days, and in a hurry. Fish swim by here all the time. Never look to the right or to the left. Never want to stop and visit."

He rolled his eyes and sighed. "Just yesterday six of my cousins took off. Begged me to come along. But I don't like to be in such a goldarned hurry any more. Besides, a body gets shoved about, this way and that. No, I need room to breathe."

He stopped chatting and wrinkled his brow. "Which reminds me. Please excuse me for a minute. Don't go away. I need a lungful of fresh air." He took off, heading for the surface of the ocean.

Sydney wondered what he was doing up there, and what a lungful of air meant. But not wanting to sound dumb, he didn't ask.

The dolphin returned soon, just as he had promised. "By the way," he said, "we need to be introduced. My name is Danny Dolphin. I used to live on the surface most of the time. You know, among humans. My job was to make people laugh and cheer when I turned somersaults in a big tank and jumped real high after red and blue rubber balls. But, as happens to everybody, I became too old to work, couldn't jump so high, wanted to take a lot of naps. So I got put back in the ocean." He scratched his stomach with his right flipper and winked at Sydney. "But I must say, it sure feels good to be back home."

Sydney thought this a fine speech, and Danny a fine fellow.

"Well, a body can't help getting older," Danny chuckled. "And anyway, I don't need as much excitement as when I was a young feller like you."

"How old are you?" Sydney asked, admiring the dolphin's nice face and big white body.

"Hey, kid. That's not polite!" Harry scolded.

32

"Oh, I don't mind," Danny said. "Young 'uns got a right to ask questions. How else they gonna learn anything? Well, I'll tell you how old I am. I'm twenty." At this, the dolphin shook his head as if it were hard to believe. "Yessir, twenty. Many migrations have come and gone since I was born into this ocean."

"Twenty?" Harry was impressed. Sydney, too. He'd heard that herring and sardines could live to the age of five. But twenty? That really was a long time.

"Yep," the dolphin chuckled again. "Don't look it, do I? I try to keep my figure, and get in plenty of swimming and leaping every day. That's how you stay young!" As if to prove it to himself, he surged upward, spread his fins, and tumbled about, blowing a few bubbles. Then he came back and said, "Pardon my asking again—my memory's not what it used to be. Where d'ja say you were heading?"

"South. To find our family in the big migration," Harry said. "We would have been with them now, but this one"— he pointed at Sydney—"got himself caught in a fishing net."

The dolphin snorted. "Fishing nets! Many's a dear friend I've lost in those nets. When them boats cut through the water and those motors roar, we dive! Fast! If I had the time I could tell you plenty of stories. Make your fins curl." His voice trailed off as if he'd had an idea. "Say, why don't you two spend the night with me in my cave? Rest up for your trip. I hunted this morning and got lots of good things to eat."

"Sounds fine," Harry said. "But we've lost a lot of time and have a long swim ahead of us. We better move on."

"Come, come," Danny said. "The little fellow is all tuckered out. Can't even keep his eyes open."

Harry had to think about it. He swam about for a moment. "Well, O.K.," he said finally. "But we've got to leave first thing in the morning."

Sydney was so relieved to hear this that he forgot he was tired.

"Follow me!" Danny shouted, then whooshed into the darkening sea. He slid past great ropes of seaweed toward a mass of boulders covered with crusty barnacles. He vanished behind them.

Harry peered into the darkness. "Where'd he go?" he asked nervously.

For once, Sydney thought he could help. Since he was smaller than Harry, he could squeeze through a wall of tiny plants to a large boulder that lay in the sand. "Come here," he yelled to Harry, who was fighting his way through the plants. "Look!"

A shaft of light from the full moon had cut through the water, showing a cave hollowed out of the base of the big boulder. Sydney, followed by his brother, swam right into its large, cozy warmth.

But all the time they were being watched. Hidden among the rotting timbers of an old shipwreck, a giant shark lay in the shadows, watching everything they did and hearing everything they said. He'd seen them with Danny, heard all about the invitation to the cave filled with delicious food.

He wasn't interested in the herring and the sardine. They were just small fry to him. He had his eye on the fat, sassy, talkative dolphin, who'd be perfect for his evening feast. Dolphin tail was a real treat, and he hadn't expected to find it in the northern waters this time of year. What luck!

But now he had to figure out how to catch it.

Following at a safe distance, he glided silently behind the herring and sardine, noting where they had squeezed through the wall of plants. He knew he could easily break through. But he had to work it so he wouldn't be seen. He'd have to pounce on them from a place they didn't expect. From inside the cave!

5

In the Cave of the Dolphin

While the giant shark watched and plotted
how to catch his prey, Harry and Sydney
found their way into the cave.

"Welcome, my friends. See you made it,"
Danny greeted them.

Enough moonlight pierced the water to
give things a warm, friendly glow. The walls
of the cave were covered with lacy strands of
green-brown seaweed. Plates of purple and

green starfish, shells of sea urchins, and the yellow, pink and red leaves of anemones lay scattered about the floor.

Sydney had never seen such a beautiful place. He saw chunks of king crab, shrimp, and other crusty bits of seafood lying on a stone shelf, and he longed to have some.

"Help yourselves!" Danny cried heartily, grabbing a large king crab in his mouth. "It's all fresh-caught this morning."

Sydney didn't realize he was so famished. He ate as fast as he could. Everything was so fresh and tasty! When he'd satisfied his hunger, he looked around some more. And that's when he noticed something strange— an opening in the roof of the cave, and a passageway that seemed to lead almost to the surface of the sea.

"I expect you're wondering what that is," Danny told Sydney. "That's an air hole, young feller. So I hardly have to leave the cave to take some nice deep breaths. I'm different from you. You can breathe through your gills right in the water. I need fresh air."

Sydney thought how different Danny was from all the other creatures in the sea, including his own family.

"As a matter of fact," the dolphin continued, "it's about time for me to zoom up there." He waved a jaunty goodbye with his flipper and eased himself up through the air hole, returning soon crunching the thick shell of a crab, which he dispatched with a snap of his jaws.

Sydney settled into a corner of the cave with the remains of his dinner. How lucky they were, he thought contentedly, to have found this warm, friendly retreat, and to have met the wonderful dolphin.

But he wasn't to feel that way long. A moment later he heard a loud, grating noise coming from the entrance to the cave.

"By Neptune!" Danny exclaimed. "What was that? No one ever visits me after dark." He darted to the entrance, paused, then returned with a worried look on his face.

"What's the matter?" Harry asked.

"Strange," Danny muttered. "Very

strange. Someone's blocked the entrance to my cave with a big rock. We can't get out."

"You mean we're trapped in here?" Sydney's voice trembled.

Danny muttered, frowned, and swished his large body back and forth. Once more he swam to the entrance and pushed his snout hard against the rock. It didn't move, not even a tiny bit. "We'll never move that thing from inside," he said. "But not to worry. I'll just swim up my air hole and scout around for help. Be back in a jiffy!"

A moment later Danny returned, a look of amazement and fear on his face. "Come and look!" he shouted. "You won't believe it!"

Harry and Sydney rushed to Danny's side. Sydney was *really* scared now. What could frighten his wise old friend so much? He followed Harry up the air hole. When his eyes got used to the dark, a horrible sight awaited him.

A huge head was wedged into the air hole, completely filling it. Nothing could get past it. The creature, whatever it was, looked furious. In fact, it was cross-eyed with rage.

40

Sydney and Harry meet Danny.

Its big jaws snapped. Its head twisted back and forth. A row of sharp, pointy teeth glinted in its open mouth.

Sydney was shocked. What he saw filled him with terror. He recognized that head! A long, jagged scar ran from the corner of its mouth down toward its left gill slit. It could only be the Great White Shark—the very same that had attacked the mackerel!

Sydney tumbled back down the air hole as fast as he could, pulling Harry along with him. "C'mon," he cried. "Let's get outa here!"

"Things sure don't look good," Harry agreed. "That's a shark, for sure. Why'd he want to come in here?"

"I don't know," Sydney said, "but now Danny can't get past him."

"And if he can't get past him . . . wow!" Harry exclaimed. "How's he gonna get fresh air?"

Danny looked worried. "I can't go without air very long," he said. "This is *some* kettle of fish! Of course, not meaning any disrespect to you fellows," he added hastily.

Sydney sank to the floor of the cave. What would happen now? He thought and thought, then remembered Mitzi's brave words when he was caught in the fishing net. "Never give up," she had said. He felt his little spine stiffen.

He swam over to the big rock blocking the entrance to the cave and searched every inch of its rough surface. If only he could find a tiny opening—just enough to squeeze through! Once he escaped, surely he would find some help.

At first he found nothing. But then he saw a thin ray of moonlight seeping through a space at the bottom of the rock. He flattened himself in the sand. "I can see out there!" he shouted.

"Good work!" Danny shouted in return. "I knew that kid had a good head on him. What do you see? I hope not more sharks."

Sydney couldn't help himself. He giggled. "They sure don't look like sharks to me. One is a funny kind of creature with a round head, big eyes, and lots of wriggly legs. The other is smaller, with a hard green shell and a long sharp claw in front. It has lots of legs, too!"

"A big fish with wriggly legs?" Danny scratched his head with his flipper. "How many?" He sank down and tried to flatten himself in the sand so that he also could peek through the opening. But he was too big.

Sydney was glad Silver Queen had taught him how to count. "One, two, three, four . . . I guess there are eight."

"Eight?" Danny asked. "Only creature I know of with eight arms—not legs—is that obnoxious Oscar the Octopus. I've warned him to keep away from my place. Probably hanging out with that friend of his, Lily the Lobster. Move over, Syd."

Again, Danny shoved and pushed his nose into the cave floor, trying to press his eye against the opening. It did not work. All he got was a mouthful of sand. He sighed. "I guess you'll have to be our eyes and ears, little one."

Sydney was eager to help, especially since Harry was looking at him with pride. He peered through the crack again. Then he pressed his ear hole against it—just in time to hear a strange conversation.

※

"Oh dear, Danny Dolphin's never going to speak to me again," Oscar the Octopus was saying, all the time rubbing a spot on the top of his head.

"Clumsy! That's what you are!" Lily the Lobster scolded. "Always were! Waving all those arms and slap-banging around. You tripped and fell against that rock, and it tumbled right in front of Danny's cave."

"Blame, blame. I get blamed for every darned thing," Oscar lamented. "I try to please. To be nice. To be sociable. To say 'howdy do' to the folks I meet. But do I get any thanks? No! Only insults. That's what I get!"

Oscar wrinkled his face. His bulging dark eyes glared at Lily. "You're the one who said, 'Let's play tag.' Not me. So now what do we do, Miss Claw? And how do we know if Danny is even in there? He's always out visiting with folks and being sociable. Maybe that's what he's doing now."

"True," Lily agreed, calming down a bit. "Tell you what. I'll just rap and see if he's home." She stretched out her long front claw and knocked three times.

✦

Inside the cave, Harry and Danny looked at one another. Three sharp knocks! What did that mean? Before Sydney could explain, Harry rushed toward the entrance and shouted, "Signals! Someone's sending us signals!"

"It's Lily the Lobster knocking to see if someone's home," Sydney said.

Harry and Danny were so upset they scarcely heard him. "It's Oscar and Lily, I expect," Danny said. But how do we answer them?"

Harry didn't know. The two of them looked glum and seemed to lose hope. But not Sydney. He began thinking. None of *them* had a long claw like Lily's, he reasoned. So they'd have

46

to use something else—something hard and sharp.

His eye lit on the many shells lying on the cave's floor. He pushed one. It rolled toward the entrance of the cave, and made a loud clinking sound.

"Well, I'll be . . ." Danny whistled in admiration. "You're a clever young man, Syd. We'll use that shell to knock on our side of the rock." With his strong tail, he slapped the shell against the huge boulder.

CLINK! CLANK! CLANK! The sound echoed through the cave. To Sydney, it sounded *very* loud. Now if only it could be heard outside! He rushed to his listening post to find out.

"Didja hear that?" Oscar yelled. "Danny's in there!" He danced about, kicking up gobs of sand.

"He's heard us all right," said Lily.

"Keep calm, Danny!" Oscar shouted at the rock. "We'll save you!" But instead of going right to work on the boulder, he sat down and unfolded his eight long arms. Next, he carefully examined the little pads attached to the bottom of each one.

"For heaven's sake!" Lily exclaimed. "Don't just sit there! Do something!"

Oscar drew himself up with all the dignity he could muster. "I'm thinking," he replied. He wobbled his round head about, waved all his arms, then stared into space.

Finally his eyes lit up. "I've got it!" he exclaimed. "You keep knocking on the rock, so Danny won't think we've left him. And I'll go for help."

"So, *that's* your big idea?" Lily sounded disgusted. "I'm supposed to sit here and bruise my claw on this rock while you go off and forget the whole thing?"

Oscar's arms went limp. "You hurt my feelings!" he said, his arms dangling pitifully at his sides. "You don't trust me." Tears began to form in his eyes.

✳

Meanwhile, inside the cave, Sydney noticed that Danny was gasping for breath. The clinking sounds he was making were growing weak. Finally he just stopped trying. He lay down on the floor of the cave and closed his eyes.

"Danny!" Sydney cried. "What's the matter?"

"Sorry young feller," the dolphin replied weakly. "Guess you and Harry will have to get out of here without me. I can't breathe. If I don't get some air soon, I'll die."

"Danny! You can't die!" Sydney pressed his little nose all over Danny's face. "Please. Please. Hold on!"

"Relax kid," Harry said confidently. "We'll think of something. No rock or old shark can get the best of us!"

Harry sounded brave, but Sydney could see that he, too, was losing heart.

Now Danny lay on his side gasping, his big body slumped against the wall of the cave. He opened his eyes and tried to manage a smile. "Don't worry about me, boys. I've had a good life. We all have to go sometime. But you two are young. Try to get out of here. Keep signalling. Lily is smarter than that dumb octopus." And with that, his head fell back on the sand.

Sydney couldn't help it. A painful sob shook him, and he buried his face in his fins. Whatever were they to do?

6

The Great Tidal Wave

Outside the cave, Lily's anger was slowly cooling. Oscar's tears had made her sorry for being so mean. She gently patted his head with her long foreclaw and said, "I trust you, Oscar. I know you'll find someone to help move that old rock. And then you'll come straight back. Now go along. I'll wait right here."

These nice words made Oscar feel better. He pulled himself up to his full height, waved all his arms, and stretched them as far as he could. "Stretch one, stretch two, stretch three," he mumbled, and then added, "I feel fine now." He pointed his head in the direction he wanted to go and crouched for his takeoff.

"Keep knocking," he called back to Lily as he disappeared in a cloud of sand.

But in their excitement, neither Oscar nor Lily had noticed that the signals from the cave had stopped.

Lily settled down in front of the big rock and resumed her knocking. One, two, three, four. She paused a moment to listen. There was no sound from inside the cave.

She began again. One, two, three, four. Still no answer.

She tried one more time. Finally her foreclaw became so sore, she stopped. She'd just have to wait until Oscar came back with some help.

She waited and waited. The minutes passed. Five minutes, ten minutes. No Oscar. She began to get mad all over again. Where was that silly, dumb octopus? Just like him to forget all about her.

But just then a long, thin form slithered toward her, leaving a skinny trail through the sand. She recognized her old friend Ernest the Eel, a discreet, middle-aged gentleman known in those parts for his wisdom about the undersea world. He wriggled up to her, stopped, and arranged his long body in a graceful curve.

"Good evening," he said in a pleasant voice.

"The same to you, sir," Lily replied. She usually only saw Ernest when the sea creatures in her neighborhood gathered to discuss common dangers—such as upcoming storms, prowling sharks, and fast-moving fishing nets.

"May I inquire why you are sitting so close to that big rock?" Ernest asked politely, gazing at her out of his big, dark eyes.

"Oh I'm waiting. Just waiting. For someone who said he'd be right back," Lily said.

"Now, who would keep a charming creature like you waiting?" Ernest asked in a soft voice.

"Well, I'll tell you who," Lily pouted. "Oscar the Octopus, that's who."

"Oh, him. I understand." Ernest rolled his eyes upward. The skin on his long slender back rippled with concern.

"We were just playing tag," Lily said, "when he fell smack against this old rock. It fell over right in front of Danny's cave. So if he's in there, he can't get out." She showed Ernest her wounded foreclaw. "I kept knocking on the rock, and for a while Danny signaled back. But now there's only silence. Oscar promised to get help, but he hasn't come back! I'm so mad!" With that, she stuck the sharp end of her foreclaw in the sand.

Mr. Eel stared at her, then at the rock. "So that nice Mr. Dolphin is trapped in his cave? Dear me. The timing couldn't be worse."

"What do you mean?"

"You haven't heard?"

"Heard what?"

"A tidal wave's coming our way." Ernest nodded his head gravely. "It could rise as high as 20 feet at the surface. And down here everything could be blown about and wrecked."

"Oh, you still believe those silly stories about the end of the world?" Lily waved her five pairs of legs in disbelief. "Good grief! I have enough problems without your making up new ones."

Ernest gazed at her sadly and shook his head. "I know it's hard to believe. But the story is true. This very morning a rumble was felt along the ocean floor. We all know what that means."

Lily chuckled. "And who told you about that?"

"The Old Turtle himself. He felt the vibrations."

Lily couldn't control her laughter. "Who'd believe the Old Turtle? He's always got his head stuck under that big shell. How would he know what's going on?"

"That shell, my dear young lady, may be tough, but it's also very sensitive," Ernest said, twitching his long body anxiously. "I beg you, my dear friend, listen to me. The Old Turtle, as peculiar as he may seem to you, has long experience with sea storms. You must find shelter." He glanced over at the cave. "Actually, this cave would do very well."

Lily noted his sincere tone of voice. "Well, maybe you're right," she sighed. "But first that rock must be moved. Oh, where in the world has that octopus gone?"

"We have no time to wait for him," Ernest said briskly. "We must act now! The big wave could be here any minute." He turned his attention to the rock. "Let's see now . . . maybe, it just might work!" He wound himself into a tight circle, then unwound, and nodded his head. "Yep. I think it could work. If I can just hit that rock at the right point, I bet it'll fall over."

"I guess it could," Lily agreed doubtfully. "But wouldn't that hurt your poor head?"

Ignoring her, the eel set right to work. First he stretched out to his full length; then he wound himself up in a tight ball. Suddenly, he shot forward, slamming his head against the rock as hard as he could.

Danger lurks outside Danny's cave.

The force of the blow made big ripples in the water, causing Lily to lose her balance. Ernest slowly uncoiled and shook himself. A big bump was already forming on his forehead.

But he didn't seem to care. He wound himself up once more—and again he shot forward. BANG! WHAM! CRACK! "One or two more times should do it," he huffed.

Inside the cave, where Danny still lay motionless, Sydney and Harry were too upset to notice all the banging—until WHAM! The rock moved! Slowly it fell to one side. The entrance to the cave was open!

"Hooray!" Harry shouted. "We've been saved. Danny's going to live!"

The brothers rushed to the dying dolphin and begged him to move, to try and swim out of the cave and float to the surface. Danny had shown no signs of life for some time. But now he moved slightly and tried to wave his left flipper. Harry and Sydney kept swimming around him, poking him with their noses and begging him to try harder.

Finally he stretched his flippers and floated toward the cave's entrance, where he nodded to the astonished Lily and Ernest, and headed upward toward the surface of the ocean.

His friends wondered if he would make it. But after what seemed like a very long time, he reappeared, a sparkle in his eyes and a fat juicy crab hanging from his mouth. "Why's everyone so gloomy?" he asked, as if nothing had happened. He offered to share his crab, doling out a succulent leg to each and everyone in the company.

The food was delicious and everybody ate heartily. Oscar the Octopus had long since been forgotten. But suddenly, just as they were finishing their meal, they saw a strange shape scurrying clumsily toward them, stirring up gobs of sand. It was Oscar.

"Hold everything! I'm coming!" he shouted. "And I brought a helper, my brother Elmer." Elmer looked a lot like Oscar, only shorter and fatter. They both slid to a stop in front of the cave and looked around in surprise. "You got out?" Oscar asked in an accusing voice. "How'd that happen? I went to a lot of trouble to rescue you."

No one spoke for a minute. Oscar glared at Harry and Sydney. "Who are you?" he shouted. "Where'd you come from?" Not waiting for an answer, he stared at the open entrance to the cave. "And who moved that rock?"

"He did," Lily said proudly, pointing to Ernest. "Almost cracked his head open to help us," Danny said, nodding respectfully toward the eel.

Oscar twitched all his arms and danced around angrily, finally losing his balance and stumbling against the rock again. But this time it did not move. His brother Elmer teetered over and helped him upright.

"I said I'd come to the rescue," he sputtered at Lily. "And I did! And this is all the thanks I get?"

"Hey, wait a minute," Harry said, swimming right up to Oscar's face and puffing out his gills. "You can't talk to a lady like that!"

"Yeah," piped Sydney. "You better cut that out!"

"Quite right," Danny agreed. "Let's show some common courtesy here." Ernest, looking very disgusted, chose that moment to be on his way. Turning to Lily, he said, "Remember my words, dear friend. Seek shelter now. The big wave is on its way." With those words, he zigzagged toward a clump of seaweed and disappeared.

Oscar scowled at the vanishing eel. "What did he mean by that?" he growled to no one in particular. "What shelter? What wave?"

"A tidal wave is due any minute," Lily replied, waving her front claw at him. "A big one. Ernest heard it from the Old Turtle this morning. The Old Turtle picked up the signals from his shell."

"From that crinkly old shell?" Oscar exploded. "And that slimy, twisting, squirming eel is spreading such a story? Lies. All lies! Besides, even if it were true, why would cranky Old Turtle confide in such a low creature? He hardly speaks to anyone except . . ."

Oscar never finished. Without warning, a mighty rush of water, churning, roaring, and thundering, surged out of nowhere. The powerful current slammed into the little party of quarreling sea creatures, hurling them against a nearby cluster of rocks.

There they clung as the huge wave heaved, billowed, and pounded at them, scattering everything in its path . . . big fish, little fish, small pebbles, great boulders, ropes of seaweed, clouds of sand. They fought to hide behind the big rocks, to no avail. Finally, with Danny leading the way, they struggled back toward the mouth of the cave—their only hope of staying alive.

At that very moment, in a nearby part of the ocean, the *Seawitch*, still laden with its big catch of fish, pitched and rocked in heavy seas. Though the worst of the tidal wave had passed, the wind and the waves still crashed and thrashed. Great walls of water washed over the little boat. Her engines, fighting the turbulent sea, whined and wheezed. Her pilot struggled to control her spinning wheel.

Out on deck, still tangled in sprawling nets, thousands of frightened fish squirmed and whimpered. Some had broken free, slipping and sliding across the rolling foredeck. They fought to get to water, tail fins beating wildly. Most never made it.

But Mitzi, Sydney's little friend, used her head. Earlier, before the tidal wave hit, hundreds of herring and sardines had been flung into fish bins, each lashed firmly to the deck. Mitzi was down near the bottom, layers of squirming fish on top of her. Little by little, though, she struggled upward, making her way to the top.

Once there she watched and waited until a giant wave slammed into the boat, rocking it wildly from side to side! Churning water drenched the fish bin, and the fish above her slid to the deck.

This was Mitzi's chance. When the next wave hit, she was ready. Riding its crest, she tumbled to the deck. And when the third wave came, she leaped, tossing and tumbling, into the sea.

The cool water flowed through her gills. She could breathe again! She swam as fast as she could away from the *Seawitch*.

But in her relief, she couldn't help wondering about Sydney. Had he made it through the storm? Would she ever see him again?

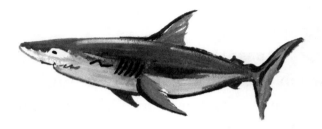

7

The Shark Trails His Prey

Meanwhile, back in the cave, Sydney and his friends listened to the sounds outside. The force of the tidal wave had slowed. The dense mass of sand and pebbles that had spun around them at the height of the storm was slowly settling to the ocean floor.

Sydney pushed his way out of the cave and looked around. Oscar Octopus wore a stunned expression. He tried moving his arms—and gave up in disgust. Lily Lobster managed to wave her sharp front claw—but ever so slowly.

Danny Dolphin shook his head and flapped his tail. He needed air. He struggled to the entrance of the cave and promptly disappeared.

Ernest the Eel, who'd rejoined his friends when the storm began, had dug a trench in the floor of the cave and buried himself. Now he was just emerging, with only his head showing above the sand.

Sydney gasped with relief. At least everybody was alive. Even the Old Turtle, who was drifting past them, wobbling unsteadily, muttered, "I told you so. I told you so."

Finally, Oscar managed to flex his arms up and down, then back and forth. He grunted with satisfaction. "They're in pretty good shape," he called to Lily, who was trying to stand up on her five pairs of legs. "What hit us?"

"I told you *before!*" she said impatiently. "The *tidal wave!* Mr. Eel spoke the truth. The Old Turtle warned him it was coming. But you wouldn't listen."

Oscar glared at her. "Nonsense!" he exclaimed. "When I see that smarty-pants eel again, I'll just smack him one!"

Ernest, clearly in no mood for a fight, started slithering from the cave, leaving a long, narrow trench in his wake. But Oscar was in a foul mood. He wobbled his way toward the eel with a menacing expression, one of his long arms set to strike.

"Hey! You quit that!" yelled Lily. "You're nothing but a big bully! Leave him alone or I'll scratch your eyes out!" Her long claw shot out, its sharp end quivering.

Sydney hated fights. He wished he could be her brave protector and confront Oscar on her behalf. But the octopus was much too big—and he was much too little.

By now, the segments on Lily's back were trembling. She thrust her claw close to Oscar's face. "You just touch that nice Mr Eel! I dare you! You'll be sorry!"

Oscar was astonished. He opened and closed his mouth, but no sound came out. Everyone in the cave watched and listened. Finally he found his voice. "Watch your words,

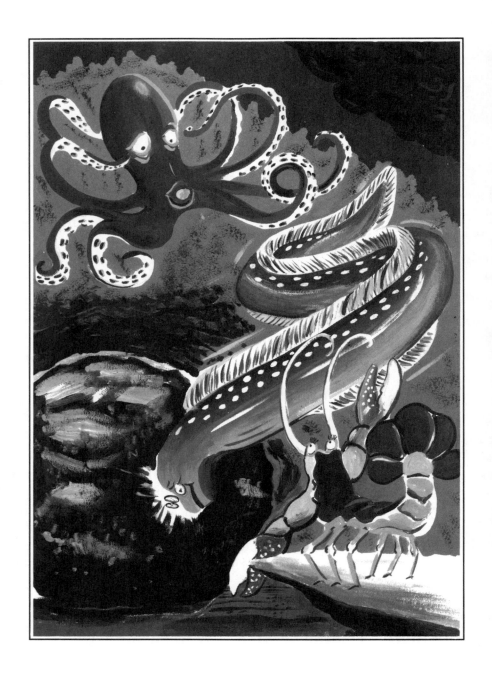

Mr. Eel makes his mark.

young lady," he sputtered. "If you like that slimy worm better than me, then let him be your best friend and see how much fun you'll have!"

Picking up a clump of sand, he threw it in Lily's face. Then he whirled about with a great flourish and teetered out of the cave.

Lily was so mad she clawed the sand with her forearm.

Feeling bad for her, Sydney swam over and planted a kiss on her head.

But as he did, he felt her quiver with alarm. He turned around to see a hard-shelled lump swimming toward them on ten fast-moving legs. Little funnels poked out from under what appeared to be a head. "What's *that*?" he asked Danny Dolphin, who had just returned—but was already cautiously backing out again.

Danny winked at him knowingly. "Better not get in its way. You'll be sorry."

"What will it do to me?"

"Never seen a squid before?" Danny asked. "You got lots to learn. If it gets mad or scared, it shoots clouds of purple ink at you. And it takes days to get it off."

By then Danny was halfway out of the cave.

Meanwhile, Harry had grown impatient. "We'd better get going," he called to Sydney. "It's getting late. We've got a long way to go before we . . ."

He stopped in mid-sentence. Oscar had come bumbling back to the cave, prancing and dancing, an apologetic smile on his face.

"There you are," he simpered to Lily. "I want to apologize. I'm sorry I threw sand in your face." He wobbled toward her, and fell right on top of the squid!

Streams of inky fluid shot out of its funnels, staining everything and everyone a deep, dark purple. Even Danny was rapidly changing color.

Harry sputtered with anger. Frantically, he tried to rub the stain off in the sand. "We shoulda been out of here long ago," he growled, looking around at his purplish-black tail.

"What happened?" Sydney shouted, watching himself grow darker.

Harry grabbed him by his fin. "Never mind what happened. Let's get going. *Now!*"

"My, my, my!" Danny was saying, looking about with a wink and a chuckle. "None of us look the same, do we?"

This reminded Harry of his manners. He swam over to Danny. "It was a pleasure to meet you, but we gotta get moving. Thanks for the good meal, Danny. Hope we see you again."

He nudged Sydney toward the cave's entrance. And in seconds they were darting away, making their way through the dark, storm-tossed sea.

"Hate to see you go," Danny called after them. "Come back any time."

✳

A short while later, Harry splashed to a halt. "I can't believe it!" he groaned. "I've lost my bearings. Which way is south?"

Sydney shook his head and shrugged. Who was he to give Harry directions? All *he* ever did was get lost.

"Hmmmmmm," Harry murmured. He turned his head to the right, then to the left. He gazed up, then down. He stretched his fins and then his tail, checking the movement of the water.

Finally he brightened. "I think I've got it!" he shouted. "The tide is pushing south. C'mon, let's go with the tide!" He waggled his tail and headed south.

Sydney plunged right after him. He dared not get lost again. But he felt sad about leaving his friends in the cave. Would he ever see any of them again—especially wise, friendly Danny?

His heart fluttered at the thought. It reminded him of his escape from the net—and the question that had nagged him ever since. Where was Mitzi? Would he ever see her again?

As Harry and Sydney sped south, thinking they'd left the cave behind, one creature they'd met there followed them, watching their every move. Lurking in the shadows, keeping a discreet distance behind them, was Great White, the shark.

How had he escaped from the cave? As it turned out, it had been easy. When the tidal wave hit, Great White, his head still hopelessly stuck in Danny's air hole, suddenly felt his body lift and float free, carried along by the rampaging waters.

He quickly righted himself and darted away.

But he didn't leave that part of the ocean. He circled around and around, watching the cave. He saw Oscar Octopus go and come back. He saw the squid release its fluid (even turning several shades darker himself.)

Finally, he saw Harry and Sydney leave.

He wasn't interested in a puny herring. Even less in a wimpy sardine. What he wanted was that big, juicy dolphin. But he was still smarting from getting caught in the air hole. Something about Harry, that smart-alecky herring—the way he'd looked up at him, his bright eyes so bold and cocky—still made

Great White's gills quiver. He'd love to swoop down on that wise guy and his sniveling little brother, Sydney, and gulp them down in one quick swallow.

There was just one trouble—keeping track of these insignificant creatures in this great, big ocean. He'd already lost sight of them. Well, never mind. He'd keep looking. Nobody ever got away from Great White.

Just thinking about it excited him. He clicked his mouthful of teeth together several times, imagining his moment of revenge.

8

Meeting up with Mitzi

Not too far ahead of Great White, Harry and Sydney maintained a steady course. For a change, the sea was calm. Streaks of ghostly fire, caused by schools of fish pulsing with electric charges, glowed eerily past them. The setting sun highlighted the drifting clouds of plankton and diatoms that floated above them.

As night fell, the waters changed from green to deep blue. A school of flounder shimmered under a faint beam of starlight. A brown, furry seal fed her baby a tiny crab she'd caught for his dinner.

That night, they sheltered under a giant rock—so huge that it thrust high above them, nearly reaching the surface of the sea. Pieces of wood and rusty metal fittings, half-buried in the sand, told a sad story. This jagged reef, unseen by boats passing over it, had surely destroyed many a hull, sending the ship and its crew to the bottom.

※

Next morning, a bright sun flashed through the water. Sydney stirred in his sleep. Had he heard a voice? Was he dreaming? He opened his eyes and saw a starfish floating by, pushing itself along with tube-like feet. A group of anchovies swam around him in circles. The voice hadn't come from them, he was sure of that. But he was just as sure that *he had heard something*.

He nudged Harry. "I heard a voice," he whispered.

Harry looked around and stretched his fins. "You must have been dreaming," he yawned.

"No, honest," Sydney insisted. "Listen." Sure enough the voice came again, a soft, moaning sound.

Harry heard it too. "Sounds like a voice all right. Wonder who it could be?"

Swimming out from under their rock, they circled around until the sound grew closer.

"Look!" Sydney cried, "over there!" The decaying mast of a sailboat, covered with barnacles, jutted from the ocean floor, its torn sail drifting up and down in the water. As they gazed at it, they heard the voice again, this time much closer.

What should they do? Poke about in the wreck? Perhaps run into danger? Or maybe help someone in trouble? They looked at each other, trying to decide.

Soon they had their answer. A small green and black fish staggered from a fold in the sail, so weak it could barely move. But when it saw Sydney and Harry, its face brightened, its fins fluttered, and its tail waved happily.

Stunned, Sydney searched the little face, hardly able to believe what he saw. It was Mitzi! Her scales were a bit bedraggled, but to him she looked beautiful.

"Mitzi? Is it you?" he called out.

"Sydney?" came a tired voice. "Thank goodness you've come!"

Sydney rushed to her, almost toppling her over in his haste. "Take it easy, little brother," Harry laughed.

"It's Mitzi, my friend from the net!" Sydney shouted. "What luck to find her!"

Turning to Mitzi, he said excitedly, "I thought I'd never see you again. When Harry and I got away, I hoped and hoped you'd escaped too. But it's O.K. now—because you're here!"

"What brought you to this spot?" Harry asked.

"After I escaped from the boat, I just swam and swam," Mitzi shuddered. "It was terrible. I didn't know where I was going. When I found this old wreck, I decided to hide in it. A little fish can't be too careful, you know."

"Certainly not," said Sydney, feeling much more worldly than when he first met Mitzi. He was such a silly kid then. But his adventures and escapes since . . . well, they just made him feel more confident.

"We want you to join us," he said. "We're heading south to find our family. Silver Queen and Big Daddy will love you. So will our sisters and brothers."

"Okay," Harry butted in, "we ought to get moving. You two'll have time to chat on the way."

The *Seawitch*, still soaked from the storm, basked in the heat of an unusually warm day. The tidal wave had dealt it a heavy blow. But now it rocked easily in calm waters, drying out in the morning sun.

Its crew sat smoking their pipes in the cabin. One of them, the pilot Jim, had a full red beard and friendly blue eyes. They gave him a hearty, jovial air. He'd been hired to help with the catch and keep the *Seawitch* off the rocks and sandbars.

The owner of the boat, Mac, was a short fellow with shifty eyes. He liked to order people around, usually in a loud, gruff voice. He was new to the sea, and he needed Jim to teach him the ropes. But it made him mad to think he wasn't really the boss—which meant he was mad most of the time.

"Must have been hundreds of herring got away in the storm," Jim said. "But we still have close to our limit. And we shouldn't go over. Taking too much means the herring die out. Pretty soon, they disappear. Let's freeze what's left and get back to port."

He looked up at the position of the sun. "If we start now, we can be there by noon."

"Nah," grumbled Mac, "we're gonna stay out another day. See if we can fill that net again." He pulled hard on his pipe. "Besides, I'll betcha there's a dolphin or two out there. I hear there's plenty around when the little fish are runnin' south." He sighed. "Sure would love to catch me one."

"If you're figurin' on catchin' dolphin," Jim said, "count me out. You know it's against the law. And besides, I like dolphins. I seen plenty of 'em, swimmin' and playin' around. They're a lot like people I reckon."

"Aw, come on," Mac snarled. "That's a lot of fancy talk. If I catch a dolphin, I know a guy who'll fetch me a good price from that Sea World place."

"Nothin' doin'," Jim said firmly. "Them critters belong in the sea." He stood up and pulled on his woolen sea cap. "I'm game for only one thing—to fill that net with herring. If we head further south, we can get out of these storms. But only small fish, ya hear? I won't help you catch no dolphin."

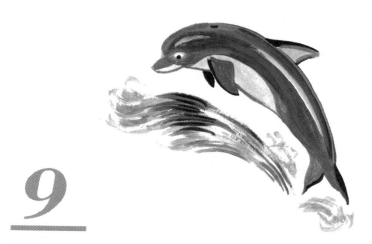

9

Piggybacking on Danny

The sun, slanting through the water, glinted on Mitzi's emerald green body, flecked here and there with shiny black markings. She'd recovered much of her strength. Her fins moved in a steady rhythm through the water, staying close to Harry. Now and then she glanced back at Sydney.

Sydney should have been swimming just as hard. But he couldn't resist showing off for Mitzi. Somersaults were his best trick. So he decided to do a few. It wouldn't take more than a second.

One. Two. Three. Four. Oops, he was feeling a bit dizzy. Maybe he'd overdone it. He tumbled back into place and looked around. Where was Mitzi? Why hadn't she been watching him? He looked again. She and Harry had disappeared! And without Harry, he didn't know where he was!

"Oh, no," he groaned. "Not again!" After all his promises to stay close and not dawdle! He whipped his tail from side to side, furious with himself. Maybe he really was a little twit, just like Harry sometimes said.

Well, he couldn't just float. If he did, he'd be sure to attract attention—the wrong kind. He swam slowly around in circles, hoping some kind creature would come along and give him directions.

Then he stopped and thought hard. When Harry was lost, he hadn't waited for another fish to come and help him. He'd figured things out for himself. O.K., that's what I'll do, Sydney said to himself. Let's see, how did Harry figure out which way was south?

Hmmmmmmmm. You turn your head to the right, then to the left. You gaze up, then down. You stretch your fins and then your tail. That should tell you which way the tide is moving. This time yesterday the tide was pushing south. *So this way should be south!*

Feeling much better, he set off, keeping up his spirits with little pep talks. Harry would be so proud of him. Mitzi would be so impressed.

✦

He hadn't gone far before he heard someone calling him. Someone coming up fast from behind. Suddenly a big, white shape splashed up beside him.

"I was sure it was you," the creature said, breathing hard. "A tiny speck alone in this big, old ocean? Who else could it be but Sydney?"

It was Danny Dolphin! He gave Sydney a big grin. "Lost again, eh?"

Sydney didn't like that one bit. Hadn't he found the way south? All by himself? Deciding to ignore Danny, he turned without speaking and swam on.

"Hey, you silly thing," Danny called after him. "Don't you know I'm your friend? Searched for you and Harry all night long. Decided I'd migrate south with you fellows after all. Hey, where *is* Harry?"

"I don't know," Sydney said, sorry he'd been so rude. "I . . . I wanted to show off a bit for Mitzi, and . . . and . . . "

"And you forgot where you were," Danny finished for him. "I can just see you trying a few somersaults. You got dizzy, right? That'll teach you a lesson. By the way, who's Mitzi?"

"She's my friend. We met in the fishing net."

"Some place to meet a lady," Danny chuckled. "Well, tell you what. I have a plan . . . "

Sydney interrupted him. "I can't swim as fast as you—if that's what you're thinking."

"Don't need to, young feller," Danny replied. "If something doesn't work one way, you think of another way. What I want you to do is hop on my back."

Sydney stared at the dolphin's big, broad back. "Go on, hop on," Danny urged. "Grab a piece of my skin in your mouth and hold on tight. You won't fall off."

How could Sydney say no? Darting onto Danny's back, he grabbed hold with his mouth and spread his fins wide to give himself balance.

"Ready, set, GO!" Danny shouted. With a joyous snort, he flipped his tail back and forth, raised and lowered his head, flapped his flippers, and whooshed off!

Sydney held on for dear life. The water streamed past, flattening the tiny scales on his back. Everything became a blur—other fish, seaweed, rocks—their colors all blending together.

Finally Danny let out a whoop. "Ahoy!" he sang out. "I think I see them. Straight ahead."

Sydney peered into the distance. Far ahead, he saw two small figures. Danny put on more speed, and in no time they pulled alongside Harry and Mitzi.

"Danny!" Harry exclaimed. "What are you doing here?" He stared at Sydney clinging to Danny's back. "And what are *you* doing up *there*? We thought you were right behind us, like you promised. No dawdling. Remember?"

"Hold everything," said Danny, raising his flipper. "When I found Sydney, he was swimming due south. No dawdling. No larking about. Just as serious and grown-up as can be."

Sydney smiled shyly and sneaked a look at Mitzi, who gazed at him admiringly.

Danny turned to Mitzi. "Sydney, this must be the young lady you were telling me about? Pleased to meetcha, Miss Mitzi."

Mitzi was clearly impressed with Danny's manners. "Pleased to meet *you*," she said, not the least bit frightened—even though dolphins are well known to snack on sardines.

"What are you doing so far from your cave?" Harry asked. "And where are your friends?"

"Ha! My friends!" Danny harrumphed. "They give me a pain in the flipper. That bumbling Oscar, he's always sniffing around for food. Sometimes, when I'm not looking, he wriggles into my cave. My very own cave, mind you! And gobbles everything in sight!"

At the thought of Oscar's eight arms, sweeping everything up off his shelves, Danny shook himself all over.

"Besides, I really missed you two," he added. "Thought I'd join you on the migration. I'm getting on a bit in years, you know. The warm waters will do me good."

"We'd love to have you," Harry replied. "And so will our parents. Big Daddy likes dolphins. Always stops and chats with them— when he's sure they've already had a good meal."

"Then it's a deal!" Danny said. "The three of you hop on my back. We'll meet up with your family in no time."

He rolled his big body to one side, and they all jumped on. Then he waggled his tail, spread his fins, bobbed his head up and down, and sped away.

Their little party hadn't gone far, though, when a deep sound rumbled through the waves. Danny stopped dead in his tracks. "What was that?" he called up to his friends.

"I don't know," Harry shouted back, acting nonchalant. But Sydney could tell he was worried. Sydney was worried, too. That sound was all too familiar.

Thundering through the water, it grew louder and louder. Finally, it was deafening. Throbbing, pulsing, pounding—until it was directly above.

"It's the fishing boat!" cried Harry.

Big Daddy and Silver Queen and their family, still traveling with the big migration, had almost reached their destination—the warm, lazy waters of the south, where each winter they enjoyed sunshine and rich feeding grounds.

But this year they felt no enjoyment. Harry and Sydney were still missing.

Silver Queen couldn't stop crying. Big Daddy tried to comfort her, but nothing he said seemed to help.

Finally, at the end of the fourth day, as they prepared to stop for the night, he hit on an idea.

"Would it make you feel any better," he said, "if we held a ceremony for our dead sons? We could build a memorial to them on the ocean floor—maybe at that protected spot behind the reef up ahead, where we always stop for the night?"

Silver Queen stopped crying and thought about that. "Yes, you're right," she said sadly. "That's what we'll do."

They settled on a quiet stretch of water sheltered by a long coral reef. The whole family fell to work, assembling a bed of seaweed, pushing pebbles together to form a small mound, and topping it with choice crab legs and brine shrimp.

Then they gathered around it, and Big Daddy said a few words. "Here's to our dear, departed sons, Harry and Sydney," he intoned, sounding very grave and solemn.

"May they swim happily ever after in the great migration in the sky."

When he finished, the family swam past the pile of pebbles and said their last farewells. Then they formed in a line and, with many a backward glance, resumed their journey south.

Only Silver Queen lingered behind. She tossed a final pebble on the mound, and when everyone was out of earshot, she whispered, "Wherever you are, my sons, remember to mind your manners, behave courteously to your fellow fish, and be a credit to your family."

When she rejoined Big Daddy, she told him, "Harry and Sydney are still alive—I just know it. They're out there somewhere. And at this very moment, they're making their way back to us."

10

Sydney Has an Idea

Silver Queen was right. Just a few miles to the north, Harry and Sydney were alive and well. But, unfortunately, they were far from safe.

The throbbing and pounding of a fishing boat could mean only one thing—the dreaded net was directly overhead!

"Let's swim away as fast as we can," cried Mitzi.

"Now wait a sec," said Danny. "Best to

think before we act. I'll swim up for a breath of air and check out the scene."

They all agreed. Mitzi tumbled off Danny's back, then Harry and Sydney. Danny shook himself and shot to the surface.

And just as quickly he was back, zooming into their midst breathlessly. "It's a fishing boat all right," he gasped. "Probably the one that caught Sydney and Mitzi in its net."

"Then Mitzi's right," Harry said. "We'd better get out of here."

But before they could move, a strange silence descended on them. The boat's engines had been turned off.

"I don't like that one bit," Danny muttered.

"Me neither," Harry said. "Let's go."

But just then the dark waters lit up. As searchlights penetrated every nook and cranny, an eerie glow revealed a giant, undulating shape. It was the hated net, weaving and snaking its way toward them!

"Time to submerge!" shouted Danny. He pointed his head downward and dove. Everyone followed.

Once settled on the ocean floor, Danny shook his head sadly. "A lot of little fish don't understand," he said. "When the fishermen drop bait—say, a big load of brine shrimp—the fish rush to eat it. Next thing they know, they're caught."

The net billowed and swirled. Under the bright lights, its webbing made grotesque patterns in the water. Down on the ocean floor, the four friends watched fearfully.

"What are we waiting for?" Harry demanded. "Are we gonna stick around here and get caught?"

"Not so fast," Danny said. "Let's see how many fish take the bait. If it's a lot, nobody's going to notice us. We can slip away unnoticed."

Until then, Sydney hadn't said much. But something was worrying him. He remembered how frightened *he'd* felt in the net. These fish must feel the same way.

He swam over to Danny's big, broad face and touched his nose with his own. "I've got something to say," he said in a firm voice.

"What's that, son."

94

"If we swim away and forget the fish trapped in the net, they'll all die."

"True," said Danny. "But what can we do? We've got to save ourselves."

"This is no time for your screwy ideas," Harry broke in. "Danny and I'll decide . . ."

"But Harry," Sydney interrupted, "you've always told me never to give up. And don't the other herring and sardines in the sea have a right to freedom—just like us?"

"The young feller's got a point," Danny said. "Take me. I don't want to be sent back to Sea World. They make you do the silliest things—catch rubber balls on your nose, wiggle around in the air, do crazy tricks on the water slide. No sirree. You won't catch a dignified old gentleman like me . . ."

"Maybe, just maybe, there's a way," Sydney broke in again, amazed at how boldly he was speaking to his elders. But he knew his idea was a good one.

In fact, it came from his own experience. Twice before he'd looked for an escape route—someplace where a small creature like himself could slip out. First, there was that time in the net; then when he was trapped in the cave. Both times he'd looked for a small opening—and failed. But he still thought it might work.

"Maybe there's a hole in the net," he said, hoping he wouldn't be laughed at. "If we could find one, we could help the fish escape. You know, swim up close and tell them to try squeezing out."

"Who would listen to you?" Harry scoffed.

"You honestly think you could swim that close and not get caught?" Danny asked. But a bit of admiration had crept into his voice.

"Why not?" replied Sydney. "Harry did it once for me. He came right up close and called out to me. Now I can do it for someone else."

Danny turned to Harry. "This brother of yours has a good heart. Plenty smart, too."

"Well," Harry grumped, "maybe he's changed. Used to be such a silly, dreamy kid."

"He's not a kid anymore," Mitzi protested, shooting a reproving look at Harry. "He's brave and wonderful. And . . . and . . . I want to help him."

That's all Sydney needed. Without a word, he pointed his head up and shot away, straight toward the dangling net.

When he reached it, he shuddered at its bulging contents. It was full of crying, wailing fish. He swam around the outside, careful to keep a safe distance. And at last he saw what he wanted. A slight tear near the bottom.

Swimming directly to it, he called to the nearest herring, who was flapping frantically about on the ropes. "Hey in there! Can you hear me?"

The herring paused. It pressed its face against the rough webbing. "Can you get us out?" it moaned. "We're being crushed to death."

"Try to be calm," Sydney shouted. "I'll do my best."

"Hurry!" the herring cried. "We won't last long."

Sydney examined the tear in the net. He took a bit of frayed rope in his mouth and began to pull. Nothing happened. He tried again. No luck. "Hold on," he yelled. "I'll get help." With that, he dove back to the bottom.

His friends gathered around him. "There's a hole all right," he told them, "but it has to be made bigger. I can't do it alone." He looked around at them. "Who will help me?"

"I will," declared Danny. "Between us, we can open up that hole."

Then, pausing, he frowned. "But darn it! With those bright lights, I'll be sure to be spotted. I do stand out, you know."

"Then *we'll* help," Harry said, swimming forward. "Mitzi and I'll go with Sydney."

Mitzi didn't say anything. She didn't have to. Everyone knew—helping Sydney was her idea all along.

Danny still looked worried. "It's not going to be easy," he said. "We'll have to distract the fishermen first, or they'll notice something's wrong with their net."

He thought for a second, then grinned broadly. "Heck, what's life without a little adventure? I'll take a few runs around the boat—you know, do a few of my old leaps. That'll get their attention. Meantime you unravel the net."

The great chase.

On the deck of the *Seawitch*, Mac and Jim were about to haul up their catch. "It's gonna be a big one," Mac called out. "We were right to stay out another . . ."

He stopped abruptly and stared over the bow. "Will ya look at that! he shouted. "Come quick! It's a dolphin! A big, shiny, white fella! We gotta catch him!"

He ran up and down the starboard rail, pointing excitedly.

Jim scowled. "I told ya before. I'm not takin' any dolphins. Leave him alone. He's not hurtin' anyone. You take that dolphin, and this boat could lose its license."

Mac pounded the rail with his fist. "You ain't got nothin' to worry about. It's my boat. Not yours!"

Jim put his hand on Mac's arm, trying to calm him. But Mac broke away. "Look at that thing, leapin' and divin'!" he shouted. "He's a good one, and I'm gonna get him!"

He dashed to the pilot house, where he locked the door from the inside and started the engine.

"Stop!" yelled Jim. "You don't know what you're doing! You'll lose tonight's catch! You'll run us aground!"

Mac laughed. You just watch me," he shouted. "I'm not lettin' that dolphin get away. I'll chase him all over this ocean if I have to!"

11

Great White Meets His Doom

Meanwhile Sydney, with Harry and Mitzi at his side, worked at the net. In a few minutes, some strands of the rope tore loose. They worked faster. The hole grew larger. Almost large enough.

As they worked, they heard the sound they'd been hoping for. The boat's engines had roared into life. Good. Danny was doing his job. The dolphin chase was on.

Something else happened, too—a piece of luck they hadn't counted on. When the *Seawitch* lurched into action, several half-unraveled ropes burst open. A big herring next to the hole popped out, then another, and another. As the boat gained speed, a whole stream of fish poured out. And by the time it disappeared, the net was empty.

Sydney looked at Harry and Mitzi, and they all doubled up with laughter. "What a joke on them," Harry cried. "We may never have managed it without their help." He laughed so hard he got a stitch in his right fin and had to stop.

"Look," cried Mitzi, "all the fish are swimming back. I guess they want to thank us." Sure enough, the entire catch was streaming toward them, cavorting with joy at being saved.

Meanwhile overhead, racing just ahead of the *Seawitch*, Danny, once known at Sea

World as Dancing Danny, performed the high-flying tricks of his youth. Catapulting through the air, snorting sprays of water through his gills, jumping high, diving low, he tantalized Mac with his antics.

Mac sped after him—zigging here, zagging there—almost capsizing the *Seawitch* in his fury.

But Danny wasn't the only large creature in those waters. A short distance behind, Great White was shooting through the sea like a bullet.

He'd started out to get even with the herring and his brother, the sissy sardine named Sydney. And at first, everything seemed so simple. He planned to stalk them for awhile, and then pounce.

But a short while back, things began to get complicated. They were joined by a tasty little female they called Mitzi—then by that fat, sassy dolphin named Danny.

He'd been content to wait, in case more succulent morsels joined the party.

But now he was getting hungry. He decided it was time to act. He streaked toward his prey, preparing to move in for the kill. Herring and sardines for appetizers, dolphin for the main course and dessert. What a feast!

But what was this? Danny was nowhere in sight. And Harry and Sydney were surrounded by thousands of confusing look-alikes! Where did all these herring and sardines come from? They looked like they'd just escaped from a net!

He hung around for awhile, cursing his fate. Then he had an idea. He'd let these three live for now. He could always come back for them later. Meanwhile, he'd find that dolphin.

He shot to the surface and looked around. And he could hardly believe his good fortune! There was that foolish dolphin, leaping about in the air. His mouth watered.

Danny was doing his specialty—the double back-flip, ending with a triple deep dive. Without a ripple, Great White glided silently beneath him. In a second or two, he would have him.

But what was this? The dolphin was acting strangely. He kept waving his flipper provocatively. At something way off in the distance. It was rapidly growing closer. A big, dark shape, plowing through the water with a deafening roar. Great White shot to the surface, hoping to get a better look. Then he froze. It was a fishing boat! And it was coming straight at him!

✶

At that very moment on the deck of the *Seawitch*, Jim threw his full weight against the pilot house door, forcing it open. Stronger and bigger than Mac, he pulled the wild-eyed little man from the wheel and grabbed it himself.

Outraged, Mac rushed down the deck, spotted the tantalizing dolphin almost under their bow, and ran to the door of the cabin where they kept a long spear gun. He'd only wound it just enough to capture it alive.

Grabbing it, he scrambled to the rail and leaned over, laughing crazily. A second later, he flung it with great force, aiming at the sleek, white creature which had just surfaced.

There was a great thrashing about in the water. The creature lunged at the boat, spouting streams of blood from a great gash in its head. It opened its wide, curving mouth and attacked the *Seawitch*, sinking long, jagged teeth into her hull.

Mac staggered back, startled by the creature's assault. He'd only meant to wound it, just enough to capture it alive. But this fellow didn't act like a dolphin. Didn't *look* like one either.

In fact, he'd never seen a dolphin with a scar running clear from its mouth to its gill!

Then it hit him. *This was no dolphin!*

"Shark attack!" he shouted at Jim. "Speed it up! We gotta outrun him!"

In the pilot house, Jim struggled to control the *Seawitch*. He pulled the wheel hard to the left, preventing her from flipping over. Then he pulled sharply to the right. The *Seawitch* continued to pitch, lurching from side to side wildly.

Mac was yelling something to him. He leaned his head out of the pilot house, straining to hear. And in that second, a mighty crunching noise rose from below. The *Seawitch* had run aground on a sand bar.

A second later, she lay half-tipped on her side, her bow tilted upward, her engines slowly dying.

The next moment, all was silence. Minutes later, Danny circled the boat, making a wide berth around Great White's carcass, which was gradually sinking below the surface. Inside Mac and Jim punched their radio, frantically calling for help.

The triumphant return

12

Back with the Family

Danny rushed back to his friends. To his surprise, he saw swarms of happy fish swimming around them, joyously swishing their fins and tails.

To his even greater surprise, he saw Oscar Octopus, waving his arms hysterically. And Lily Lobster, snapping her front claw reprovingly. And Ernest the Eel, reclining in a perfect figure eight. And the Old Turtle, peering warily out from his shell.

"We just got here," Lily explained. "We were lonesome after Danny left. The old neighborhood just wasn't the same. So we decided to migrate with you. The Old Turtle carried me on his back."

She turned pleading eyes to Danny. "Please, can we come?"

Danny looked at Harry. Then at Sydney and Mitzi. They gave him the fins-up sign.

"Sure you can," he said. Everyone, including their thousands of new friends, showed their support with a round of applause, delivered by blowing bubbles in the water.

⋅✦⋅

They arrived at the family's southern resting grounds the next morning. The largest contingent, the herring led by Harry, extended as far as the eye could see. The sardines, almost as large, followed close behind.

Bringing up the rear were the four old friends—Oscar, Lily, Ernest and the Old Turtle—traveling as fast as dozens of arms and legs, a cumbersome shell, and a long, slithery body could take them.

But the main attraction of the day was Sydney. Up at the head of the line, riding proudly atop Danny's broad back, he led the parade as Grand Marshal. Mitzi occupied an equal place of honor beside him.

Danny tried to act properly dignified, in keeping with his age and importance. But now and then he couldn't resist a little leap.

At sight of them, Silver Queen burst into tears. But this time she cried for joy. "I knew it," she exclaimed. "I knew they were still alive."

Big Daddy, after hearing of their adventures, said he always knew Sydney would grow up to be a hero.

Harry immediately made plans for a party. He rounded up dozens of his brothers and went in search of food. When they returned, laden with brine shrimp and fresh plankton, Big Daddy swam to the head of the lagoon, raised his right fin, and announced with great fanfare: "Let the revelry begin!"

Far into the night they frolicked in the warm southern waters, singing and dancing and feasting. But to Sydney, what mattered most was that he was home, surrounded by friends and family.

"Adventure," he said to Mitzi, "is fine when you're still a kid. But there comes a time when a sardine must think of other things. Like starting his *own* family."

Mitzi nodded her head wisely.